CHADRON STATE COLLEGE

CYPCo
56657

W9-BTC-700

E
H493r

ROSALIE

Story by Joan Hewett

ROSALIE

Pictures by Donald Carrick

Lothrop, Lee & Shepard Books　　New York

Text copyright © 1987 by Joan Hewett.
Illustrations copyright © 1987 by Donald Carrick.
All rights reserved. No part of this book may be reproduced or utilized in any
form or by any means, electronic or mechanical, including photocopying,
recording or by any information storage and retrieval system, without permission
in writing from the Publisher. Inquiries should be addressed to Lothrop, Lee &
Shepard Books, a division of William Morrow & Company, Inc., 105 Madison
Avenue, New York, New York 10016. Printed in Japan.

First Edition
1   2   3   4   5   6   7   8   9   10

Library of Congress Cataloging in Publication Data
Hewett, Joan.   Rosalie.
    Summary: Cindy still loves to talk to and play with her dog Rosalie, even though
her pet is very old and in poor health. [1. Dogs—Fiction] I. Carrick, Donald, ill.
II. Title. PZ7.H4485Ro   1987   [E]   86-7333
ISBN 0-688-06228-8   ISBN 0-688-06229-6 (lib. bdg.)

With love to
Dick, Angela, Chris, Karen, and Juliet

J. H.

To Ginger

D. C.

"You're sixteen years old now," I tell Rosalie. "Sixteen! The vet says that you'd be close to a hundred years old if you were a person."

Rosalie looks at me. She doesn't bark, or even wiggle. Of course Rosalie is deaf and doesn't hear me. But dogs don't understand about age anyway. And besides, Rosalie doesn't feel that old.

She's always ready to play when I am. She doesn't run fast, and now and then she stops to rest. But she wags her tail to keep the game going, and then she chases me some more.

Everyone speaks to Rosalie just as though she could hear. "It's me, Cindy," I call to her when I get home from school. If she's not there to meet me, I find her and wake her.

"Hello, Rosie," my brother Greg says.

"Hello, Rosie," his friends all say.

Rosalie's tail goes round and round, and she stays and plays.

But sometimes she falls asleep, and Greg and his friends forget that she's there. If she gets hit or stepped on, she squeals and the game stops. Then everyone lets Rosalie know that they're sorry. And Rosalie lets them know that it's all right.

It takes a while for people to see how cute Rosalie is. At first my friend Alex didn't even like Rosalie. But now she loves her.

Almost every day, when there's nothing left to try on and we've finished playing, we take Rosalie for a walk.

"Remember, she can't hear the cars coming," my mom says.

"When you're holding Rosalie's leash, you're the boss," my dad says. And we nod and stand a little taller.

Rosalie knows when we're going hiking. She watches hopefully. Sadly. And when we get back, she sniffs us so hard it tickles. Greg remembers when Rosalie went along on hiking trips. She would lead the way, run on ahead, then climb a cliff to watch us come.

We get out the family photos, and there are pictures taken a long time ago when Rosalie was young and sleek. She almost doesn't look like Rosalie.

RETA E. KING LIBRARY
CHADRON STATE COLLEGE
CHADRON, NE 69337

When friends and relatives visit from out of town, Rosalie greets them and they say, "Why, it is...It's Rosalie." They're always glad to see her. They sound surprised and kind of proud when they add, "Rosalie remembers me!"

Rosalie likes to snooze in the sun, by the door. "What a watchdog!" Mr. Foy, our next-door neighbor, says whenever he comes over.

Sometimes Rosalie doesn't feel well and can barely walk. We take her to the vet.

The vet can't cure her, but he gives her an injection to make the pain go away. And he gives my mom pills for Rosalie to take if the pain comes back. Then he asks if Rosalie has been getting her vitamins. My mom says, "Yes, one each day."

Rosalie is always eager for a treat, and she knows when I have a biscuit in my pocket. She follows me about and reminds me that she's there.

When my dad sees her begging, he shakes his head. "Just because Rosalie is old, there's no reason to spoil her," he says.

Rosalie's not allowed on the furniture. But once in a while, when the whole family is sitting together, an odd thing happens. My dad beckons Rosalie over and picks her up. My mom pretends not to notice. And Rosalie sits among us, smiling.